Native
American
Peoples

HOPI

Mary Stout

Gareth Stevens Publishing

A WORLD ALMANAC EDUCATION GROUP COMPANY

Please visit our web site at: www.garethstevens.com
For a free color catalog describing Gareth Stevens Publishing's list of high-quality books
and multimedia programs, call 1-800-542-2595 (USA) or 1-800-387-3178 (Canada).
Gareth Stevens Publishing's fax: (414) 332-3567.

Library of Congress Cataloging-in-Publication Data

Stout, Mary, 1954-
    Hopi / by Mary Stout.
      p. cm. — (Native American peoples)
    Includes bibliographical references and index.
    ISBN 0-8368-4218-9 (lib. bdg.)
    1. Hopi Indians—History—Juvenile literature. 2. Hopi Indians—
Social life and customs—Juvenile literature. I. Title. II. Series.
    E99.H7S86   2004
    979.1004'9745—dc22   2004046687

First published in 2005 by
Gareth Stevens Publishing
A World Almanac Education Group Company
330 West Olive Street, Suite 100
Milwaukee, WI 53212 USA

Produced by Discovery Books
Project editor: Valerie J. Weber
Designer and page production: Sabine Beaupré
Photo researcher: Tom Humphrey
Native American consultant: Robert J. Conley, M.A., Former Director of Native American
   Studies at Morningside College and Montana State University
Maps: Stefan Chabluk
Gareth Stevens editorial direction: Mark Sachner
Gareth Stevens art direction: Tammy West
Gareth Stevens production: Jessica Morris

Photo credits: Corbis: cover, pp. 5, 8, 10, 11 (top), 12, 17, 18 (bottom), 22, 26, 27; Peter
Newark's American Pictures: pp. 6, 7, 14, 16, 20 (top), 23 (both); North Wind Picture
Archives: p. 9; Native Stock: pp. 11 (bottom), 18 (top), 19, 20 (bottom), 21, 24.

Printed in the United States of America

1 2 3 4 5 6 7 8 9 09 08 07 06 05 04

Cover caption: According to one Hopi story, each group of people coming from the under-
world to wander the earth in search of a home was accompanied by an old woman of great
wisdom. Today, Hopi grandmothers, such as this one, are important figures in Hopi life.

Contents

Chapter 1: Origins 4

Chapter 2: History 6

Chapter 3: Traditional Way of Life 14

Chapter 4: Today 22

Time Line 28

Glossary 29

More Resources 30

Things to Think About and Do 31

Index 32

Words that appear in the glossary are printed in
boldface type the first time they appear in the text.

Origins

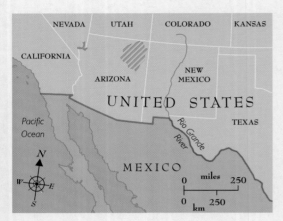

The orange area on this map shows the Hopis' homeland before it became part of the United States.

The Peaceful People

The word *Hopi* has been defined as "peaceful people," "righteous," or "virtuous." The westernmost group of **Pueblo Indians,** the Hopis live on a 1.6 million-acre (648,000-hectare) **reservation** in northeastern Arizona. Slightly smaller than the state of Rhode Island, it is a limited portion of their traditional lands and completely surrounded by the Navajo Reservation. The population of the Hopi Reservation in 2000 was 10,645, with the people living in fourteen villages on top of three **mesas:** First Mesa, Second Mesa, and Third Mesa.

Scientists have proven that the Hopis have lived in this area for at least one thousand years. Most believe that the Hopis and other Native Americans are descended from people who came from Asia across the Bering Strait. They walked over a landmass that may have stretched between what is now Asia and Alaska during the Ice Age that ended about ten thousand years ago. Others think that the original Native Americans came by boat to South or Central America and walked up to North America.

The Traditional Hopi Origin Story

Many Hopis believe that they came to this world, called the Fourth World, from another place beneath this world — called the Third World — long, long ago. According to Hopi traditional beliefs, Tawa, the Sun Spirit, created all the people. Gogyeng

Called "the oldest people" by other tribes, Hopis have lived for centuries in the dry, open countryside called the Black Mesa in Arizona.

Sowuhti, known as the Spider Grandmother, and the boy warrior gods, Pokanghoya and Polongahoya, led the people with good hearts into the Fourth World. Evil people were left behind. The good people climbed a reed through a hole in the sky. They found the Fourth World empty except for Masauwu, the god of fire and death, who welcomed them.

Yawpa, the mock-ingbird, divided the people into different tribes. After bringing light and warmth to the Fourth World as instructed by Spider Grandmother, these tribes traveled to find their homes. The Hopis settled in an area that is now called Black Mesa, Arizona.

∿ The Hopi Language ∿

About five thousand people speak the Hopi language at home. Here are a few words:

Hopi	Pronunciation	English
tsiro	tsi-roh	bird
taaqa	tay-kwah	man
kiihu	kiy-hooh	house
kwaahu	kway-hooh	eagle
kuuyi	kooh-yih	water
tusqua	toos-kwah	land

History

A Long History in a Dry Land

For 850 years, Hopis have lived in Oraibi, Arizona, the oldest surviving settlement in the United States. In Oraibi and other villages, the Hopis farmed corn, using methods that produced successful harvests in a desert land. They mined coal and used it for firing pottery, cooking, and heating. The people built **kivas**, underground rooms, for complex ceremonies created to insure Hopi survival. They also defended themselves against raids by Navajos and other Native American tribes.

The Spanish Come and Go

In 1540, Hopis in Oraibi's neighboring town of Awatovi met the Spanish explorer Pedro de Tovar, sent by Francisco Vásquez de Coronado to find gold. De Tovar discovered the Hopis had no gold and returned to Zuni in New Mexico to rejoin Coronado.

Coronado and his soldiers crossed the southwestern United States in search of the fabled Seven Cities of Gold in 1540 at the request of the king of Spain, who had heard rumors of great riches north of Mexico.

In 1629, three priests arrived in Awatovi and built a Christian **mission** there, but the priests had little effect on Hopi traditional beliefs. However, the people in the mission introduced sheep, cattle, fruits, vegetables, and metal tools to the Hopis.

In 1680, the Hopis joined with other Pueblo peoples in the Pueblo **Revolt** against the Spanish, who counted the region part of the Spanish Empire in Mexico. Twelve years later, the Spanish once again conquered the Pueblo peoples of New Mexico. Priests returned to Awatovi, causing disagreement among the Hopis. Some wanted to live like the Christians, and others wanted to continue to live in the traditional manner. In 1700, the traditional Hopis killed all the Christian men and destroyed Awatovi. From 1823 to 1845, the Mexican governors located in Santa Fe, New Mexico, failed to stop Navajos and other Native groups from raiding Hopi **pueblos**.

The Pueblo Revolt

Pópe, a **medicine man** of the San Juan Pueblos, organized the 1680 revolt against the Spanish. During the mid-1600s, the Spanish had moved into New Mexico and built missions in all the Pueblo towns. Tired of living with the Spanish people, who treated them as workers and servants and forced them to follow their religion, the Native Americans were ready for a change. Pópe sent messengers to all of the Pueblo peoples, including the Hopis, telling them to fight the Spanish on the same day. Since there were no calendars, Pópe sent a cord with knots showing how many days until the revolt. Although the Pueblos' revolt was successful, the Spanish soon returned.

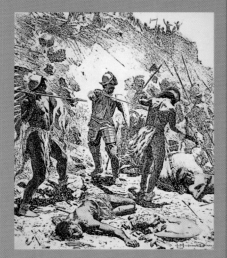

During the Pueblo Revolt, Native Americans killed the Spanish or chased them out of town and destroyed everything that was Spanish.

American Contact

In 1846, the United States and Mexico began a war over which country held present-day Texas and the location of that state's boundary with Mexico. When the United States won the war in 1848, it gained a vast amount of territory, including Texas, California, Nevada, Utah, and most of Arizona as well as parts of other present-day U.S. states. Hopi lands thus became a part of the United States.

Hopi men traveled to Santa Fe, New Mexico, to ask John Calhoun (above), Indian agent and later governor of the territory, for help in defending themselves against Navajo raids.

In 1849, the U.S. government named John Calhoun to act as Indian agent and govern the southwestern tribes. The Hopis began to meet American missionaries, traders, explorers, government officials, and tourists. In 1874, the Keams Canyon government agency was built, as were three Christian missions. Without consulting the Hopis, President Chester Arthur established a reservation, where all members of the tribe were supposed to live, in 1882. However, the new Hopi reservation covered only one-tenth of their traditional lands.

The creation of a **boarding school** at Keams Canyon in 1887 had a huge effect on traditional Hopi society. Hopi children were forced to attend the school, where they learned the English language and American customs. During the same year, Congress passed the Dawes Severalty Act, which required Native American tribes to divide their reservation and give each family one piece of land. The traditional Hopis fought against this law, and many of them were sent to prison. In the end, the Hopis kept their reservation whole and did not split it up.

Two traditionally dressed Hopi girls sit in a window in 1900. The American boarding schools did not prepare Hopi girls and boys for their life on the reservation.

Keams Canyon Indian School

The children attending Keams Canyon Indian School were forced to cut their hair, wear American clothing, and speak only English. Separated from their families and culture for years, they were not allowed to participate in Hopi ceremonies. The food and rooms were terrible, and many Hopi children caught diseases and died. Many Hopis refused to send their children, so the government sent soldiers to force the children to go to school and to arrest their parents. Because of the terrible conditions there, the boarding school, which had opened in 1887, was shut in 1915.

Edward S. Curtis's photographs documented traditional Native American life across much of North America. He took this haunting photo of a traditionally dressed Hopi man from the village of Walpi in 1906.

Early Twentieth Century

During the early 1900s, disagreements among the Hopis created the worst problems the tribe had yet faced. Hopis divided into two different sides: the U.S. government reports named them the "Friendlies" and the "Hostiles." The Friendlies were in favor of learning English and cooperating with the government. Today, they are called "Progressives." Called the "Traditionalists" today, the Hostiles did not want any changes to the Hopi lifestyle.

In 1906, the disagreements between the Hostiles and the Friendlies of Oraibi ended in a fight. Youkeoma, leader of the Hostiles, drew a line in the sand and said that he and his people would leave Oraibi if the Friendlies' leader, Tewaquaptewa, could push him across the line. After a long pushing contest, he was pushed over the line, and the Hostiles left Oraibi to begin a

A President Values Hopi Culture

President Theodore Roosevelt visited the village of Walpi in 1913 and was very impressed with the people, their lifestyle, and their ceremonies. He wrote about the Hopis, expressing appreciation for their unique culture. In an article published in 1913, Roosevelt said, "It is to be hoped that the art, the music, the poetry of their elders will be preserved during the change coming over the younger generation."

The traditional Pueblo Indian architecture of Old Oraibi featured an adobe and stone "apartment building" where Hopis could climb to the top floor by stone stairs or by ladder.

new traditional village called Hotevilla. Oraibi continued to lose people until it became a dying village of only one hundred people instead of a lively center of six hundred.

The 1934 Indian Reorganization Act provided a way for Native American nations to establish their own tribal government; each voted whether to accept the act. Though most Hopis refused to vote in the tribal election, the Hopi Tribal Council was formed in 1936. The council functioned only occasionally until the 1950s.

Present-day Hotevilla features modern housing funded by the U.S. government.

Later Twentieth Century

With World War II (1939–1945) came an increase in the number of Hopis moving off the reservation. Some fought in the war, while some **conscientious objectors** left the reservation to provide other services to the country, such as nursing, fighting fires, or building dams. Still others left the reservation to work in factories to aid the war effort. Most of these Hopis returned to the reservation more knowledgeable about the outside world.

The tribal council was revived in the 1950s to deal with the outsiders, such as U.S. government officials and other non-Hopis, but the twelve Hopi villages each governed themselves. All but one of the villages favor the traditional Hopi form of government by a *kikmongwi*, or village chief.

During World War II, Private Floyd Dann, a Hopi, spoke to other tribal members in the U.S. Army using a code based on the Hopi language. No one on the enemy side could figure out what the Hopis were saying, making this a useful way of passing information during wartime.

Hopi Conscientious Objectors

The Hopis have always tried to peacefully resolve conflicts without going to war. During World War I (1914–1919), only 10 percent of the Hopis served in the armed forces; the rest of the tribe held on to their tradition of peace. Many Hopis registered as conscientious objectors during World War II. Although most signed up to serve the government in ways that did not involve combat, many others were put in prison because they refused to fight. Today, Hopis are allowed to become conscientious objectors in any war because of their deep and long-held tradition of peace.

One of the first things that the new tribal council did was to sue the Navajo tribe in 1960. The Hopis claimed that Navajo settlers trespassed on the Hopi Reservation as established in 1882 and that the land belonged to the Hopis. This problem became so large that the U.S. government passed the 1974 Navajo-Hopi Land Settlement Act. This law divided the disputed land between the Navajos who lived there and the Hopis who owned it. Hopis who lived on Navajo land were supposed to move to the Hopi land, and the Navajos on Hopi land were to move to Navajo land. While most of the Hopis left Navajo land, many Navajo families on Hopi land did not, having lived there for generations. Both sides are unhappy with the current situation, and **negotiations** continue. The Hopis deeply feel the loss of even more of their traditional lands.

It is upon this land that we wish to live in peace and harmony with our friends and with our neighbors.

From the 1951 Shongopovi village leaders' statement to the federal Bureau of Indian Affairs about the Hopi traditional lands

Traditional Way of Life

Hopi Economy and Lifestyle

The Hopis were farmers, growing corn, beans, squash, and cotton. After they met the Spanish, they traded these crops for animals such as horses and sheep, as well as for peaches and apricots. They also traded with the people from Mexico for chili peppers.

Each Hopi village took care of its own people. There was no **private property**; different **clans** owned the fields along the waterways below the villages. While the fields belonged to the women in each clan, their husbands, brothers, and sons planted and cared for the crops.

The Hopis planted at least twenty-four different kinds of colored corn but most often used the blue and white kinds. Many wild plants growing nearby proved useful for making shampoo, hairbrushes, brooms, baskets, and trays. The Hopis hunted rabbits and other small animals and traded for other goods that they needed, first with other tribes and later with the Spanish and the Americans.

Hopi men hunted rabbits with a curved stick that was thrown with deadly accuracy at the racing cottontails.

Hopi men contributed their work in the fields, the harvests, and their sheep to the household where they lived — their mother's, wife's, or sister's household. They also wove material, usually for ceremonial clothing of white cotton and wool, while the women made pottery. The women also ground the corn and cooked a variety of meals with it. One of the most common foods was called *piki,* a paper-thin bread made of blue corn that was cooked on a special hot piki stone found in every Hopi household.

Social Organization

All Hopi people belonged to a clan, a group of relatives of a person's mother. Hopi households contained just one family but often included the mother's other relatives. Originally seventy-five clans existed, but today there are thirty-four Hopi clans, including the Cloud, Spider, Snake, Bear, Butterfly, and Eagle clans. Each clan has its own **kachina** (a form of spirit being) and special responsibilities in the village and during ceremonies. Clan members always knew what their roles in Hopi society were.

Hopi Homes

Attached to other Hopis' homes, the typical Hopi home was made out of adobe. As in an apartment building, walls separated each family's living space, often with several rooms upstairs and downstairs. The downstairs rooms were storage rooms, and the family lived in the upstairs rooms and cooked piki on the roof of the storage rooms. Inside the cool, shady rooms was space for weaving, sleeping, eating, and family life. Ladders on the outside of the home led to the roof, where people could sleep if it was too warm inside.

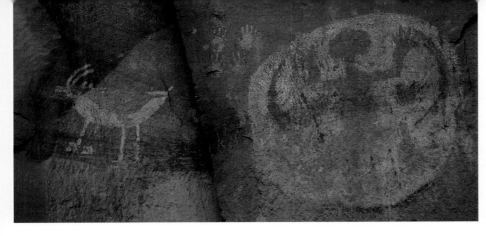

The left-hand image in these rock carvings at Betatakin, a cliff village in Arizona, represents the Hopi fire clan.

Hopis also belonged to societies made up of members of various clans. There were fewer societies than clans. Members of the societies were leaders for the important ceremonies; they made sure that the ceremonies were performed correctly and that each clan did their part. Important ceremonies such as *Soyal* (the winter **solstice** ceremony) had their own societies to govern them, and all adult men belonged to the Kachina Society as well as at least one other society.

Each Hopi village was independent and governed itself. Typically, the village chief, or kikmongwi, chose and trained the next leader, but the villagers had to approve the choice. Usually the head of the Bear Clan, the kikmongwi led the village, solved

Kachina Discipline

When Hopi children seriously misbehaved, their parents didn't ground them. Instead, when the children least expected it, scary-looking kachinas — carrying ropes, axes, and baskets on their back to hold the children — arrived at the door to take them away. These kachinas told everyone about the children's bad behavior and threatened to eat them. Parents hurried over to give the kachina food to eat instead, and the children promised better behavior.

problems, and worked with outsiders. The Second-in-command, the village crier, called out the news and announcements as he walked through the village each morning.

A Child's Life

Families hid their babies from the sun for nineteen days after birth. On the twentieth day, the baby's grandmother named it in a family ceremony. The baby was then blessed with cornmeal and taken outside to meet the sun at dawn.

Children learned how to do things by helping their parents with household work. They might begin by gathering firewood or helping adults pick fruits and plants. Soon the boys learned how to hunt rabbits, grow corn, and weave cloth. The girls learned how to grind corn and make piki bread, baskets, and pottery. Children spent time playing games such as running races, shooting arrows, and throwing darts. Adults told traditional stories to teach children Hopi history, religion, culture, and the proper way to behave.

This Hopi mother and child are all dressed up to visit Hopi House. Relatives in the mother's clan also help teach the child how to be a good clan member.

One of the Museum of Northern Arizona's exhibits is a life-sized kiva ceremonial room, such as those used by the Hopis. The Hopis climbed down ladders into the kiva, which represented the world from which the people had emerged long ago.

Both boys and girls were **initiated** into a society at age seven, where they were given another name. The boys were able to enter the kivas after that. When girls were ready to marry, they had a corn-grinding ceremony and put their hair up into a special "squash-blossom" style over their ears. They wore it this way until they were married. Adolescent boys had a second initiation into one of four societies — singer, horn, agave, or *wuwuchim* (which means New Fire Ceremony) — sometime between ages sixteen and twenty and began to participate fully in Hopi ceremonial life.

A Hopi girl's hair is arranged into the special "squash-blossom" style that she wore until she was married, when she would wear it loose or in braids. Today, young women wear this time-consuming style only on special occasions.

Adult Life

Women wore a *manta,* a blanket wrapped around them and fastened like a dress. In cool weather, men wore shirts and pants; when it was warm, they just wore **breechcloths**. When it got cold, everyone put on leggings and blankets.

When a man and woman were married, the man's male relatives wove the bride's wedding robes out of white cotton, and the bride ground corn for the groom's family for four days before the wedding. After the marriage ceremony, where the groom's parents washed the hair of the bride and groom in a yucca-root shampoo and everyone had a large feast, the bride and groom went to live with the bride's family.

Kachina Dolls

According to traditional Hopi religious beliefs, kachinas were supernatural beings who come to Hopi villages from February through July each year to participate in Hopi ceremonies. They had the power to bring rain, help the people, and punish anyone who deserved it. People thought of kachinas as messengers from the gods.

On ceremonial-dance days, adults dressed as kachinas also brought gifts to the boys and girls. Girls usually received a brightly painted, carved wooden doll that looked like a kachina, and boys received colorful bows and arrows, rattles, or **bullroarers**. The girls' dolls have become popular with tourists and collectors. Today, many talented Hopi carvers create kachina dolls for sale.

Most Hopi men carve different kinds of kachina dolls out of the roots of cottonwood trees and paint them.

The Hopis have a complicated cycle of ceremonies occurring each month throughout the year. This picture, made in 1910, shows dancers in the plaza during a Hopi harvest ceremony, which was probably one of the women's ceremonies in September.

Hopi Ceremonies

Most ceremonies were held to honor and communicate with the spirits, asking for life, rain, and good crops. In the Hopi desert country, everything depended upon rain, and this was reflected in their ceremonial life.

Organized in the villages, the important ceremonies lasted for eight or more days. The first part of most ceremonies included secret rituals performed in the kivas. Involving the public, the second part of the ceremony happened in a central plaza and was more festive.

According to traditional beliefs, Hopi kachinas are spiritual beings, wearing masks like this one, who come from afar to dance in some ceremonies.

Some ceremonies were women's ceremonies, and some were social events. The Hopi societies put on the ceremonies, but certain things could only be done by specific clan members; for example, a man of the Sand clan had to bring sand to make the altar in one ceremony.

Ceremonies started when the village crier called everyone to gather. Many times, offerings of feathered prayer sticks, or *pahos*, were placed on altars and in other sacred places. Many of these ceremonies continue today.

Snake Dance

One of the most famous Hopi ceremonies is the long, complicated Snake Dance. This ceremony begins with members of the Snake Society gathering snakes from the desert and bringing them into the kiva for prayer. According to traditional beliefs, the snakes are messengers to the gods and spirits living in the worlds below. The snakes are washed to purify them, and then men from the Antelope and Snake societies dance around the plaza, holding the snakes in their mouth. At the end of the ceremony, the men release the snakes into the desert. Traditional Hopis believe that the animals bring prayers for rain from their mouths to the ears of the gods and spirits.

Hopi men are chosen to go out into the desert and collect every snake that they come across and bring them into the kiva.

Today

Contemporary Hopis

Children living on the Hopi Reservation are raised in a traditional manner in their homes, but they attend regular schools just like other children. Although they learn English, writing, and math at school, they may still speak Hopi at home and participate in the Hopi societies when they are old enough. All children are involved with their parents in a busy round of Hopi ceremonies and

The Hopis raise their children with a strong emphasis on tradition, balanced with an equally strong emphasis on education. In 2001, the nation set up a $10 million fund to help pay for Hopis to attend college.

Lori Ann Piestewa

Lori Ann Piestewa was the first female Native American soldier to die in combat while serving in the U.S. military. This twenty-three-year old Hopi mother of two children from Tuba City, Arizona, was driving a Humvee, a boxy, armored car, for the 507th Maintenance Company when it was attacked on March 23, 2003 during Operation Iraqi Freedom. Though Piestewa could have driven to safety, instead she courageously drove up and down the line of vehicles, stopping for others who were stranded. A rocket hit her Humvee, and she was killed. The State of Arizona changed the name of a mountain in Phoenix to Piestewa Peak to honor Lori Piestewa.

This Second Mesa woman uses traditional techniques and designs to make coiled baskets and trays for tourists.

must learn the differences between over two hundred different kachinas.

Even though Hopis continue to live a traditional lifestyle on the reservation, many young people leave the reservation to find work elsewhere. The Hopis are still known for being peaceful people, but young people sometimes take advantage of the jobs provided by the U.S. Army.

Those Hopis who do not have jobs off the reservation might work at the Hopi Cultural Center, a modern complex with a hotel, restaurant, and many craft shops. Others work at the trading post or for the reservation health service or may be teachers or police officers on the reservation. Many make crafts to sell to tourists. Men carve kachina dolls, craft silver into lovely objects, or weave cotton. Women of each mesa specialize in a craft: the First Mesa women make pottery, Second Mesa women weave trays with yucca, and Third Mesa women form trays from colorful wicker.

Using an overlay method, Hopi silversmiths cut a design from a thin layer of silver and place it over another piece of silver.

Hopi Arts and Literature

The Hopis have always had a rich and varied artistic tradition, which continues to this day. Kachina doll carving has remained a strong artistic tradition among the Hopis, and many men carve these representatives of the Hopi spirit world.

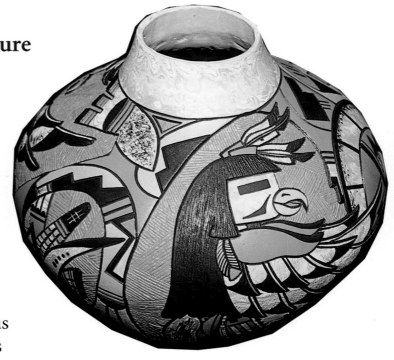

Made from the clay found near the First Mesa, Hopi pottery features three colors patterned in traditional designs.

One of the most famous Native American potters is Nampeyo, a Hopi-Tewa. Born in 1860, she began making clay pots at a time when the Hopis were starting to use American factory-made pottery. Nampeyo's use of ancient Hopi designs turned the useful pots into beautiful art; her pots are the only ones from that time recognized and collected as art. She was a potter-in-residence at the Grand Canyon's Hopi House and inspired many potters who came after her.

Wendy Rose is a well-known poet, **anthropologist**, and scholar. She often writes poems that explain her search for her roots. Her father, a Hopi, and her mother, a Miwok-European, raised her in Oakland, California, in a nontraditional manner.

Like butterflies made
to grow another way
this woman is chiseled
on the face of your world.
The badger-claw of her father
shows slightly in the stone
burrowed from her sight
facing west from home.

Excerpt from a Wendy Rose poem, "To Some Few Hopi Ancestors"

24

Charles Loloma, Jeweler

Born in Hotevilla on the Third Mesa, Charles Loloma (1921–1991) was a member of the Badger clan. He went to Phoenix Indian School, where he worked with painting and ceramics. Loloma became interested in making jewelry and experimented with Hopi designs in silver. He used many different types of stones such as turquoise, diamonds, and pearls as well as bones in his jewelry. Inspired by the shapes and colors of his homeland, he developed his own unique style. Fresh and new, his work was rejected at some art shows because it didn't look "Indian" enough. Today, if you ask Native American jewelers whose work they most admire, the answer will probably be "Charles Loloma."

Current Hopi Issues

As with many other Native American nations, the independent Hopi Nation faces the very large issue of continuing their traditional culture. Because they remain isolated from today's American culture on the remote Arizona mesas surrounded by the Navajo Reservation, they have been more successful than most tribes. Though many Native American tribes have raised money for their people by owning **casinos**, the Hopis have decided not to build one on their reservation, believing that gambling is not the Hopi way. However, these factors have led to a situation where there are few jobs on the reservation, and young people often leave to find work elsewhere.

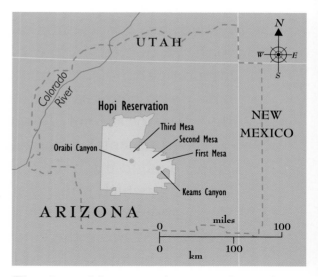

The dotted lines on this map show the boundaries of the Navajo Reservation, which completely surrounds the Hopi Reservation shown in yellow.

Today, many Hopi boys love basketball and other sports, but they also learn to run for miles over the mesas in preparation for their traditional ceremonial duties.

One remaining source of income — tourism — remains controversial. Tourists are a good source of income for hotels, restaurants, and kachina carvers, but they are very disruptive to the Hopi lifestyle; many Hopis don't like to have tourists attending their ceremonies and festivities. In fact, some villages have posted signs saying that white outsiders are not allowed in the village or are not allowed to attend Hopi ceremonies.

Environmental issues also concern the Hopi Nation. The Hopis depend upon the income from the Peabody Coal Company, which mines coal at the Black Mesa. However, they worry about air pollution from the smoke of the coal-burning **generator** plant in the Four Corners area and the increasing use of their only source of underground water.

The Hopis are also upset that some non-Hopis pretend that they know about Hopi religion and try to get money or attention by sharing this knowledge. The Hopis say that their religion is complicated and secret, and they are not supposed to share information about it. The true Hopis are practicing their religion on the reservation and teaching their children about it. They are working hard to keep the Hopi culture alive by continuing their traditional language and religion.

Hopi Water Crisis

There are no rivers or lakes on Hopi lands; Hopis depend upon rain for farming and wells for their water. They get their drinking water from the Navajo Aquifer, which is an underground body of water beneath Black Mesa. Peabody Coal Company has been mining coal from the Black Mesa since 1970, using water from the same aquifer to move the coal through a 273-mile- (440-kilometer-) long pipeline to be used at a generator plant in the Four Corners area. Peabody Coal uses 120,000 gallons (462,000 liters) of water an hour, and the Hopis fear that they are running out of water in their desert homeland. They are asking the company to find another way to transport their coal to the power station, and they are working with others to build a water pipeline from Lake Powell in Utah to their homeland.

Soon, the traditional Hopi farming method of using only rainwater to irrigate crops may not supply enough food for all of the people. Farmers are looking for other water sources.

Time Line

1540   Spanish explorers arrive in Hopi villages.

1629   First Christian mission built at Awatovi.

1680   Hopi population is 2,800; Pueblo Revolt ejects Spanish from area.

1821   Mexican independence from Spain; Hopi lands belong to Mexico.

1848   U.S. and Mexican War; Hopi land now belongs to the United States.

1874   Keams Canyon Agency and three Christian missions built.

1879   Hopi population is 1,790.

1882   President Chester Arthur establishes Hopi Reservation.

1887   Boarding school at Keams Canyon built.

1906   Hostiles leave Oraibi after a fight and start a new village, Hotevilla.

1913   President Theodore Roosevelt visits the Hopi at Walpi.

1915   Keams Canyon Indian School shut down.

1918   Hopi population is 2,285.

1936   Hopi Tribal Council first formed.

1950   Hopi population is 3,500.

1970   Hopi Nation signs a lease with Peabody Coal Company.

1974   Navajo-Hopi Land Settlement Act divides disputed land between peoples of the two tribes.

2000   Hopi population is 10,645.

2003   Lori Ann Piestewa is the first female Native American U.S. soldier to die in a war.

Glossary

anthropologist: a scientist who studies peoples and their cultures.

boarding school: a place where children must live at the school.

breechcloths: strips of cloth worn around the hips.

bullroarer: small flat piece of wood attached to a string that makes a loud noise when whirled around by the string.

casinos: buildings that have slot machines and other gambling games.

clans: groups of related families.

conscientious objectors: people who refuse to become soldiers because of their religious or moral beliefs.

generator: a large machine that creates electricity.

initiated: with a special ceremony, given permission to enter a certain group and share secret information.

kachina: a powerful spirit that sometimes appears on earth.

kivas: special underground rooms that are used only for religious and ceremonial purposes by men.

medicine man: a healer and spiritual leader.

mesas: wide, flat mountain tops with cliffs on each side.

mission: a church or other building where people of one religion try to teach people of another religion their beliefs.

negotiations: discussions to reach an agreement on a problem.

private property: land or objects that belong only to one person.

Pueblo Indians: a group of different Native American tribes who live in the Southwest.

pueblos: Native American villages in the Southwest.

reservation: land set aside by the government for specific Native American tribes to live on.

revolt: a rebellion or uprising against rulers.

solstice: two days during the year when the Sun reaches the farthest north or the farthest south.

More Resources

Web Sites:

http://www.hopi.nsn.us The official web site of the Hopi tribe contains information on history, customs, games, current political issues, and other aspects of Hopi life.

http://www.nau.edu/~hcpo-p/index.html The Official Hopi Cultural Preservation Office Home Page includes information on various Hopi crafts, history, agriculture, beliefs, and links to other useful sites.

http://www.canyonart.com/kachina.htm Go to this site for an explanation of Hopi kachinas and images of the traditional art.

http://www.hopiart.com/kach-exp.htm A guide to Hopi kachinas.

Videos:

Hopi Prophecy. Films for the Humanities, 1994.

Siskyavi: The Place of Chasms. Electronic Arts Intermix, 1989.

Winds of Change. A Matter of Choice. PBS Video, 1990.

Books:

Landau, Elaine. *The Hopi* (Native Peoples). Franklin Watts, 1994.

Lassieur, Allison. *The Hopi*. Bridgestone Books, 2002.

Santella, Andrew. *The Hopi*. Children's Press, 2002.

Sears, Bryan P. *The Hopi Indians* (The Junior Library of American Indians). Chelsea House Publishing, 1994.

Secakuku, Susan. *Meet Mindy: A Native Girl from the Southwest*. Beyond Words Publishing, 2003; Gareth Stevens Publishing, 2004.

Smith, Roland. *The Last Lobo*. Hyperion Books for Children, 1999.

Sneve, Virginia Driving Hawk. *The Hopis* (A First Americans Book). Holiday House, 1995.

Things to Think About and Do

Make a Bullroarer

Get a thin piece of wood that is 1.5 inches (4 centimeters) wide and 6 inches (15 cm) long. Drill a hole in the center of one end and thread cotton string about 3 to 4 feet (0.9 to 1.2 meters) long through it and knot. Take brightly colored tempera paints and paint designs on the wood. When the paint has dried, pick up the string and carefully whirl the wood around your head; you'll be surprised at the sound.

A Letter Home

Pretend that you have been sent to a boarding school in a foreign country where they will not let you speak your language or wear your regular clothes or hairstyle, and you cannot celebrate the holidays that you know. Write a letter home to a friend, parents, or brother/sister, and tell them the things that you miss the most.

Debate

Divide a group of people in half. One side are Friendlies, the other side are Hostiles. Each person should tell why he or she does or does not want outsiders to attend the ceremonies in their Hopi village.

Flash Card Kachinas

Using an additional reference book or the web sites listed in this book, find pictures of about a dozen kachinas. Draw and color pictures of the different kachinas, and paste them onto one side of an index card. On the other side, write the name of the kachina and something about it. Using your flash cards, see how quickly you can learn to identify different kachinas.

Index

Arthur, Chester A., 8
arts and crafts, 19, 23, 24, 25, 26
Awatovi, 6, 7

beliefs, 4, 7, 17, 19, 21, 26
Black Mesa, 5, 27

Calhoun, John, 8
ceremonies, 6, 9, 10, 16, 18, 19,
  20–21, 22, 26
clans, 15, 25
clothing, 9, 19
conscientious objectors, 12, 13
cooking, 6
culture, 10, 15, 17, 25, 27

education, 8, 9, 22
employment, 23, 25

family life, 17–19
farming, 6, 14, 17, 27
food, 15, 17

gambling, 25
government, Hopi, 11, 12, 13,
  14, 16
government, U.S., 8, 10, 12

Hotevilla, 25
housing, 15
hunting, 14, 17

kachinas, 15, 16, 19, 23, 24, 26
kivas, 6, 18, 20, 21

language, 5, 22

Mesas, First, Second, and Third 4,
  23, 25
mining, 6, 27
missions, 7, 8

Nampeyo, 24
Navajos, 4, 6, 7, 13, 25

Operation Iraqi Freedom, 22
Oraibi, 6, 10

Piestewa, Lori Ann, 22
Pópe, 7
Pueblo Indians, 4, 7
Pueblo Revolt, 7

reservation, 8, 12, 13, 22, 23, 25, 27
roles, 14, 15, 16–17
Roosevelt, Theodore, 10
Rose, Wendy, 24

societies, 16, 18, 21, 22
Spanish, 6, 7, 14

Tewaquaptewa, 10
tourism, 23, 26
trade, 14

water, 26, 27
World War II, 12, 13

Youkeoma, 10